IN-BETWEEN

AN ARKOMA STORY

ALEX LEVERETTE

I ♡ Coffee
Culture!

authorHOUSE®

AuthorHouse™
1663 Liberty Drive
Bloomington, IN 47403
www.authorhouse.com
Phone: 833-262-8899

Published by AuthorHouse 11/16/2021

ISBN: 978-1-6655-4477-1 (sc)
ISBN: 978-1-6655-4475-7 (hc)
ISBN: 978-1-6655-4476-4 (e)

Library of Congress Control Number: 2021923481

*To my friends and family, who throughout my life,
have become one in the same.*

*Also to me, because part of me never
thought I'd make it this far.*

PREFACE

Arkoma. One of the last cities out there in the wasteland. This steampunk dystopia was once thought to be humanity's last bastion of hope in the world, before being completely overrun and destroyed by the rich company owners, who further polluted the ever-declining environment.

Rather than solving this issue, the rich humored an alternate course of action. To dig a massive cavern underneath the Surface City, and rebuild. Converting the Surface's factories into air purifiers, this new high class utopia could survive centuries, despite the dying world above.

The issue with that?

It seems they didn't quite dig enough to fit everyone.

POLVO STOOD IN FRONT of the elaborate wooden desk. As he walked into the office before, he took notice of the detailed carvings and inlays along the beautiful piece of furniture. The gorgeous desk almost made up for the ugliness inside the man that sat behind it.

"Mr. Poplip. Your father says you are of use to the company. I would consider it to be your utmost priority *not* to prove him otherwise."

Polvo stood with his hands gripping each other behind his back. His teeth gritted as he stared into the eyes of the CEO. He unclenched his jaw and spoke as clearly as possible.

"Are you saying you don't trust my father, sir? Despite having worked with him since the beginning of your career?"

It was the CEO's turn to grit his teeth.

"You seem to misunderstand, Polvo. Your father, I

trust. *You,* on the other hand, are *not* your father. Now, I'll ask you explicitly. Are you, Mr. Poplip, of use to my company?"

Polvo rarely thought of people other than himself, but in that moment, Dorothy Vorgund fought her way into his head. Her family's little shop on the corner of Burns Street and GearLock Boulevard, where he spent so many days as a kid. That shop was on the surface. Now, as he stared Don Gorov in the face, he stood in the top floor of the GoroCo skyscraper, the first completed building of the Undercity.

"Well?" Gorov said impatiently. Polvo blinked his thoughts out of his head and refocused his eyes on the Don.

"Yes, sir. I am of use to your company."

2

"POLVO, COME *ON!"* DOROTHY** yelled as she slowed down her pace as they ran. "You're *way* too slow today!"

She eventually stopped, and let the heavily wheezing Polvo catch up. "It's... not fair..." Polvo said in between his deep breaths. "You're just... older than me."

Dorothy laughed loudly as she walked with him towards the shop again. "Only by a year," she said as she smacked him on the shoulder. Polvo shook his head as he continued panting. "Who knew... when you go from eleven to twelve... your strength grows so much..."

Dorothy laughed again, this time Polvo joined in. Making her laugh, intentionally or unintentionally, was one of his favorite things to do.

As the two finally reached the shop again, Dorothy's parents smiled at the two kids. Polvo's parents, on the other hand, seemed to sneer more than grin.

"Come on, Polvo," his mother said as she grabbed his hand and pulled him into walking with her. "It's time we get going now."

Polvo turned back to Dorothy and waved. She looked sad, but she waved back.

"Momma, why can't I play with Dorothy more?" Polvo looked up at his mother as they walked alongside his father. His father laughed to himself as he lit up a cigarette.

"We can only spend so much time around those kinds of people, Polvo," she explained.

Polvo's nose scrunched up in confusion. "Why not? They're no different than us, aren't they?"

His father laughed again, louder this time. Polvo loved making Dorothy laugh, but when his father did it, he only felt cold.

"No, honey, they aren't the same as us," his mother continued. "They don't have as much money as us."

"What does that have to do with anything?"

The three of them stopped walking. His mother knelt down to Polvo's eye level. "Listen, hun. They don't have as much money as us. That means, they eat worse food, wear worse clothes, and live in worse places. We're done with this conversation, I'm getting a headache."

Polvo just nodded at his mother. He knew when she got like this, that's pretty much all he *could* do. As the family started walking again, Polvo looked around at the other vendor stands and shops. He looked up to his mother to see if she was watching. She hardly ever was. He reached out casually with his hand and plucked a piece of jewelry from a vendor as they walked past. The feeling in his heart, and the rush in his mind as he stole felt addictive, and he knew it meant no good.

3

POLVO WALKED AS CLOSE to the ground as possible. He hid behind shop tables as he listened to the worker walking on the other side of them. A wicked smile spread across his face, and he felt the usual rush of adrenaline in his chest when he stole from places. He listened intently on the footsteps of the vendor as they varied in volume. When they were just right, Polvo leapt from behind the stand, and shouted as loud as he could.

Dorothy yelped and almost tripped on a table behind her, before Polvo grabbed her hand to keep her from toppling over. Polvo cackled as Dorothy's face flushed red, and a scowl appeared on her face.

"Polvo, you *idiot!*" She shouted, before eventually smiling.

"Long time no see, huh girlfriend?" Polvo said as

he hopped over the table and embraced Dorothy in a warm hug.

"Polvo," She said again. "You idiot."

"So!" He exclaimed as he let her go. "Wanna take a break? Go for a walk?"

Dorothy looked to her mother, who was sitting in her usual chair in the back of the shop. She just waved her hand at the two without looking up from her newspaper. Dorothy and Polvo smiled at each other, and walked swiftly out of the shop.

"So, what've you been up to? How's moving?" Dorothy started the conversation as they walked along the street.

"Ah, you know, it's whatever," Polvo said as he interlaced his fingers behind his head and looked up at the smoke-ridden sky. "Parents are more stressed than ever, and being underground is kind of… interesting."

"It'll work out fine I'm sure! From what you described to me, the Undercity will be huge! It's obvious that you'd be one of the first to move down there though. Your parents are pretty loaded."

Polvo made a pouty face at the mention of his parents. "I hate those guys, man. Business this, business that. Money this, money that. That's all they talk about."

"I mean," Dorothy slowed her pace as they walked. "That's kinda what runs the world."

"Yeah, you're right, but I don't want to have to think about it all the damn time."

"Fair point."

There was a brief silence between the two teenagers as they walked together. Dorothy's eyes traced the buildings they walked past, while Polvo's were locked on the sky above them.

Suddenly reaching a main street, Dorothy stopped. It took Polvo a second to notice, but he eventually stopped too, and broke his eye contact with the smoke in the sky. Dorothy's eyes stared in the distance down the road, at one of the massive construction sites leading to the Undercity.

"Is it true, Polvo?" She broke the silence. "That it's big enough for everyone?"

Polvo stared at her and felt the blood rushing to his cheeks. He clenched his jaw for a moment, before taking a quiet deep breath.

"That's what the plan is," he lied. "Overheard my dad talking with one of the construction leaders. They're saying they're going to expand the underground in waves, moving in sector by sector from the surface."

Dorothy smiled and looked back at him.

"That's amazing, isn't it?"

4

"**P**OLVO, WHERE ARE YOU** going?" Polvo's mother asked. Polvo rolled his eyes as he opened his front door.

"Just running errands, mom. I'll be back later," Polvo said as he took his first step outside.

"We have enough groceries though, Polvo," his mother said loudly, causing Polvo to stop in his tracks. "You better not be going to the surface," she said, tapping her foot. "You know you aren't allowed."

Polvo gritted his teeth. "Fine, mom. I'm leaving now." He closed the door a little bit harder than usual behind him. He despised his parents, now more than ever. The company owners' police force had been restricting access to the surface city, but Polvo could always get past them. His parents, on the other hand, not so much.

Looking up at the ceiling of earth far above him,

Polvo sighed as he started walking through the artificial city streets. He reached into the bag on his back and pulled a respirator out as he slipped into a familiar back alley. There was a small half-door that usually had a valve to open it, that led to the surface, but today, the valve wasn't there. Polvo looked briefly around the alleyway to see if it had just been cast aside, but with no luck. Eventually, he grabbed a stray piece of piping on the ground, and jammed it into the door's broken valve stem.

A few labored twists, and the door swung open. A cloud of cool air rushed over him. It felt refreshing, but he was glad he still had his respirator on. Without it, he would've probably been left coughing for the next hour or two.

He took a few deep breaths, testing out the respirator, before bending down and walking through the door. The tunnel to the surface was pretty steep, and stretched upwards for what felt like way too long. Polvo knew the limits to the rich's technology. He knew they couldn't have dug the area for the Undercity and started construction in the span of time that they claimed to have. There were clearly plans to do this that emerged long ago. The whole thing seemed way too staged.

Polvo shook the thought from his head as he pushed

the door to the surface open. This door opened just offsetting the Main Street of the Calm Waters, one of the new districts on the surface city. He had used this door many times before though, and he set off in the direction he always did. Straight to the Economy Hub. Straight to Dorothy.

5

THE SUITED MAN HURRIED his way into the main office. He gripped his clipboard tightly in his hands as he stared at the back of the Boss's leather chair. "Don Gorov," he managed to choke out. "The construction has been going amazingly. The factories on the surface seem to be converting to our air purifiers quite well."

The massive leather chair spun around, and Don Gorov stared the small man in the face.

"Spare me the numbers. Just tell me, will we meet our timeframe?"

"W-Well, sir..." The man started.

"You *do* know," Don Gorov interrupted. "That if we do not meet that timeframe, then we can't fully seal off the city."

The man looked down at his clipboard nervously. Don Gorov pinched the bridge of his nose with his fingers.

"Don't you dare tell me that we haven't found a way to deal with the people blowing them up."

"S-S-Sir… the Sewers gang members have proven to be… elusive, to say the least," the man stuttered uncomfortably.

Don Gorov slammed a fist down on his desk. The man in the suit flinched violently.

"If we are forced to delay the seal of the Undercity, more of our lives are at stake. You *know* about the air quality up there. It's only worsening. Now find a way to stop those fucking *Rats* from blowing up our factories!"

The man in the suit enthusiastically agreed, and left the room as fast as he could. Don Gorov sighed and leaned back in his chair. He sat in silence for a moment and closed his eyes as he thought.

"Kill the Rats. How can we kill the fucking Rats…"

Before long, another man in a suit pushed the office doors open. Don Gorov pinched the bridge of his nose once more. He pivoted in his chair and prepared another session of yelling, but when he opened his eyes, he saw Travis Poplip, loosening the tie at his collar.

"Travis!" Don Gorov exclaimed. "To what do I owe this pleasure?"

"Yeah, I'm still thinking on that," Travis said, breaking eye contact to stare at the ground. He gritted his teeth.

Don Gorov sat forward in his chair. "What's bothering you?"

Travis sighed, and sat in the chair in front of Don Gorov's desk. The businessman behind the desk lifted the cap out of a decanter of alcohol, and poured two glasses. Travis took the glass closest to him and sipped the liquor.

"It's Polvo. He's been sneaking to the surface."

Don Gorov's eyebrows pushed upward as he sipped from his glass.

"Well," he started after a pause, "We can't have that, can we?"

"No, we can't, G."

Don Gorov took another sip from his glass and put it down. He clicked his tongue. "Welp. He won't have much more time to be doin' that… Either way, I'll have a team of guys around your place. Keep things nice and tidy."

Travis breathed a labored sigh. "Thanks, G. You know I wouldn't come to you if it wasn't important."

"Spoken like a true Ex-C.F.O."

Travis loosened his necktie again and stood up. He turned towards the door and started walking.

"If you decided to come back, you know I'd let you," Don Gorov called after him.

"Yeah," Travis said as he pushed the door open. "I know you would."

6

POLVO SIGHED AS HE picked up some of the various things on sale at the shop.

"What's up? You seem lost in thought. And I didn't think you thought about much," Dorothy snickered and gave Polvo a little bump on the shoulder. Polvo sighed again, and put down the item he was holding. He opened his mouth to reply, but hesitated as his attention was grabbed by the shelves. Dorothy's brow furrowed as she looked at the shelf as well. The whole thing was shaking.

In fact, the whole store had begun shaking.

Polvo and Dorothy looked around, a little frantically, and moved in different directions. Dorothy towards her mother, and Polvo, out of the shop. Looking past the buildings, towards the center of the city, he covered his mouth in shock as he watched the plume of smoke billow into the sky. Running back into the shop, he helped Dorothy and her mother hold onto shelves so they didn't fall over.

The shaking didn't last long, and as it slowed to a stop, the three inside the shop relaxed their tensed muscles a bit. Polvo and Dorothy looked to her mother and made sure she was alright. She just nodded, and slowly walked back to her desk. Polvo motioned for Dorothy to follow him outside, and the two pushed the doors open.

Walking outside again, Polvo looked to the plume of smoke, which had only gotten bigger. Dorothy's gaze followed the direction of Polvo's, and her hands covered her mouth just as fast as Polvo's did.

"What is that?" She managed to break the silence.

"I... don't know," Polvo said shakily. He had a few speculations, but none of them were good. "Listen, D, I gotta go check that out. Do you want to stay here and help your mom?"

Dorothy broke her gaze at the smoke and met Polvo's eyes. "That... That might be the best move," she spoke nervously.

"All right," Polvo said as he planted a kiss on her cheek and started walking towards the city. "I'll be safe. No worries."

"You better be!" She called after him as he turned and started running. She stood there for another few seconds and rubbed her cheek, before snapping out of it, and running back into the shop's entrance.

⋘◆⋙

As Polvo got closer to the city, the smoke in the air got thicker and thicker. He reached into his bag and grabbed for his respirator mask. His parents had gotten him one of the newer models; a prototype, actually. Eventually the plan was to have a tube that connects to an external oxygen tank directly built into the mask, but without it, it still had the air filtration technology. The only downside was that it basically covered his whole head.

Securing the mask over his head, Polvo hastened his pace as he ran. He realized that as he ran now, he encountered more and more people frantically running in the opposite direction.

Eventually, he reached it. The laughter rang out through the air as the crowd of people threw trash and rubble at the burning skeleton of a factory.

The Sewers.

Polvo quickly ran behind a building and looked out at the crowd of people. They all had the same respirator. One of the first models released, so they weren't the best, technologically speaking. Stitched onto the end of each mask was the long, grey snout of a rat. Some even had little teeth sticking out of the bottom. He heard one of the gang members scream, *"Just like Filthus!"*, and another, *"Long live the Sewers!"*

The Sewers was a gang created years ago, built upon the ideals of devaluing the rich in the city. Their creator, Filthus, was a homeless nomad, who gained the appreciation of many by single handedly blowing up one of the hundreds of factories in the city. The idea of destroying anything that helped the rich, inspired many of the impoverished citizens of the city to join Filthus' newfound cause. Eventually as time went on, and the more smoke that entered the sky, life expectancy gradually went down by a decade or two, and Filthus eventually reached that threshold. Upon his death, the crown of the 'Rat King' was passed to one of the many followers, who went by the name of Nezumi.

Polvo stood in horror, staring at the destruction of the factory. Around the time Filthus died, the Sewers gradually stopped their destruction of factories, as security measures got more and more advanced. It seems as though the transition to living in the Undercity meant less people guarding them now though.

One voice rang out louder among the crowd of laughter. Polvo's eyes looked at the man standing atop a massive piece of rubble. The golden crown glittered in the light of the fire behind him. He threw the tools he had in his hands to the ground, and raised his arms above his head. He screamed at the crowd, and the crowd screamed back. This was the Sewers. This was Nezumi.

"DAMN IT!" DON GOROV** slammed his fist down on his desk. "*Another* factory today, huh?"

The businessman standing across from him shook violently. Don Gorov stared at the wooden inlays on his desk, and listened to his own breath in his ears. He gritted his teeth as he slammed the desk once more, and stood from his chair. Spinning around, he walked to the window behind him and stared out at the developing city beneath him.

"S-Sir... it seems as though there's nothing for us to do... What with the security being moved down here in preparation for-"

"I *KNOW* what they're preparing for. I know. I made the plans. That was me. What I *don't* know, is how I'm going to put an end to these fucking Rats."

The man stared at his shoes. "I don't know either sir."

"And you're damn lucky you aren't being paid to

know. Because you'd be on the Surface again, faster than you could ever know," Don Gorov paused for a moment, and turned to the man. "What *are* you paid to do here?"

The man swallowed, and adjusted his collar. "Information relays, mostly. I suppose a modified secretary, if anything, sir."

Don Gorov calmed himself for a moment. He smiled and pushed his brow up a bit. "Well, you're doing a bang-up job so far. Try getting me some good news sometime, huh?"

"Y-Yes, sir," the man said, before he quickly turned, and exited the room. Don Gorov stood in silence for a couple minutes, thinking, before moving back to his desk, and opening a few binders. His eyes scanned the papers inside for a while, and he eventually started going through different binders, looking for something.

Eventually, he snapped his fingers, and opened one of the many desk drawers. Pulling out a small, black book, he pried the cover open, and smiled, before snapping the book shut, and walking out of his office.

<hr />

Travis Poplip sat in his office, reading. He sighed, and felt his aging muscles relax into the back of his chair. He sipped a cup of warm liquid, and smiled as he reached his peace.

There was a loud knock at the door. Travis spilled a few drops of his beverage, and sighed once more. This time, an annoyed sigh. He gently closed the book, and stood from his chair. He stretched a little before walking down the flight of stairs, and walking to the living room. His wife stopped as he came down the stairs; as she was already on her way to the door. Travis smiled warmly, and told her to go back to whatever it was she was doing. His wife smiled back, and walked into the other room. Travis' peace was interrupted, but he was still happy. He walked to the door. He had a great life, a great house, a great family. He opened the door.

"Travis!" Don Gorov exclaimed, and proposed a handshake.

Travis' peace had officially been interrupted.

"G," Travis said hesitantly, as he took the man's hand and shook.

"May I come in?" The large man asked as he looked past Travis' shoulder, into the house.

"Yeah... I suppose," Travis stood aside, and Don

Gorov stepped into the house. He took a deep breath, and smiled as he looked the whole interior over.

"Love what you've done with the place, Travis! Absolutely love it," he trailed off.

Travis pinched the bridge of his nose. "Listen, G, we don't need this formal greeting shit, just tell me what's up."

Don Gorov stared at the ground for a moment, before nodding, and taking another breath. "I need your help."

Travis' eyebrows jumped up for a second.

"Listen. Another factory was destroyed today. I don't know what the fuck to do anymore. If any more get destroyed, the sealing of the Undercity could get delayed... indefinitely."

"Maybe that's what should happen," Travis said with a snappy tone. Don Gorov raised his finger and pointed at the man standing across from him.

"Don't think you can say that, as if you aren't one of the rich sons of bitches *living* down here, you fuck."

Travis was trying to prepare another comeback, but couldn't find the words. He stood and stared at Don Gorov. He hated nothing more than admitting he was right, but for once, Don Gorov had the upper hand on him.

"What do you need, G?"

Don Gorov smiled. "I remember your talents with a blade. More than most, I'd say," he said as he rubbed his forearms, and then the side of his waist. "And I know those skills haven't deteriorated over this time. Listen, what I need from you, is an end to your retirement. I need you back, and I think you still owe me for everything I've given you."

Travis stared daggers at Don Gorov. "No," he said abruptly. "No, I can't. I can't do it."

Don Gorov took a step towards him, and began to raise his voice. "Oh, I think you *can,* and I think you *will.* Because you *owe* me, Travis. You *owe-*"

"Polvo," Travis interjected. Don Gorov's foot froze mid step for a moment, before he put it down again at his side.

"What?"

"Polvo… My son… He can help you."

Don Gorov's face split into a sinister smile. "Really?" He said loudly. Travis could see his wife peeking from the other room. "You'd *really* sell out your own *son* to me, before coming back to work?"

Travis gritted his teeth. "Yes," he said plainly, after a while.

"Well," Don Gorov said, looking at the stairs, and then around him. "Where is he then?"

"On the surface," Travis said through his once again gritted teeth.

Don Gorov clicked his tongue, and started towards the door. Opening it, he paused, and looked back at Travis. He still had his book in his hand. "Ah, almost forgot," Don Gorov said as he reached into his coat pocket. "If you're going to be reading, I'd say catch up on this," He said as he tossed the little black book to Travis.

Travis caught the book with his free hand, and looked at the blank cover for a moment. Looking up again, he saw Don Gorov out the door, and beginning to close it behind him.

"Send your boy to me once he's back down here," he said as he closed the door.

Travis stood, frozen. He dropped his other book onto the coffee table below him, and cracked the black book open. The first page was blank with the exception of two words.

THE TEMPEST.

8

"**R**IGHT THEN, MR. POPLIP,**"** Don Gorov said as he stared down at Polvo, who stood in front of the massive desk. "Let's clarify that one more time for the people in the back," he chuckled. "You *are* of use to me?"

Polvo stared sternly at Don Gorov. "Like I said before," he ground his teeth together. "Yes."

Don Gorov's face split into a wicked smile. "Good, good. Let's get you started then, hm?" The huge businessman stood from behind his desk, and called out into the lobby. Soon after the call, the office doors swung open, and four people walked in. Polvo broke his eye contact with Don Gorov and looked to the oncoming group.

"This," Don Gorov broke the silence. "Is your gang, Mr. Poplip. You'll operate under the alias of The Tempest. Cutting straight to the point, you'll be stationed on the surface, and your entire goal will be to combat The Sewers, you know, keep them from blowing up all of my shit."

A couple of the people among the crowd groaned at the mention of the surface, but as Don Gorov glared out at them, they all quickly hushed once more.

"Right, so, standing here, including Mr. Poplip, is only a mere five people. Don't let the people up there know that. Act as though you're only the grunts, working for a big home of operations, which is located elsewhere. If you let people know how limited you are, you'll lose all sense of power and influence. Another thing, there are already plenty of established gangs up there. You're gonna need to be flashy to gain traction. Flashy, meaning sinister, of course. You need to publicly kill people. Lots of people. Taking all of your histories into account, I know you won't necessarily have too many issues with that."

A brief silence dawned on the group as they took in everything Don Gorov had said. Polvo was frozen. Petty theft as a way to act rebellious to your parents is one thing, but going up there and killing the very people you spent your childhood with… That was something else entirely.

"And another thing," Don Gorov broke the silence once more. "If you find anyone that wants to join the cause, let them. Once they join, tell them they'll need around a year of experience before you let them into the home base. Either that or make up something better. Basically, we need them to join the gang to help us with the Sewers, but we also can't let them know that we aren't really a gang. You get the picture."

The group remained silent. They basically stood in anticipation of Don Gorov's next words. The man looked out to them all and nodded to himself. He plopped himself back into his chair, and clapped his hands loudly. "Right then. The fucking Rats blew up another one of my factories today, so you guys are going up first thing tomorrow morning. Meet at the main gate once you wake up. Take this time to introduce yourselves to each other now. Just... outside my office... meaning leave now."

At that, the group walked out the doors behind them. Polvo remained for a moment, staring at Don Gorov. There were a thousand things he could've said; that he *wanted* to say, but he didn't. He took another moment, and turned towards the door.

"Good luck, Mr. Poplip," Don Gorov said to Polvo as he walked out of the office. "And have fun."

Stepping out of the office, Polvo looked to the other four people, who looked back in silence. One eventually broke the group's silence. "Fucking bullshit," he said angrily, drawing the attention of the group. He was tall, and his short brown hair was groomed perfectly. His eyes were a boring brown, and he was dressed nicely. He undid his collar, and loosened his necktie. "My family worked so hard to get down here, and now I have to fucking go right back up. Gorov better *know* I'll kill people."

"You'll just be doing what he tells us at that point," a girl said, drawing the attention of the group. She was short, and wore round, neat glasses. She had a big tuft of curly orange hair that sat atop her head. "How did he even pick out who was forced into this group?"

There was a dull murmuring amongst the group as they each gave their various hypotheses. Eventually, another younger man spoke above the crowd. He was a bit shorter than the other one, but he had long blond hair. He wore a thick black headband around his forehead, and looked not so confident in talking. "Let's just take turns introducing ourselves, yeah? I figure if we're forced into this thing together, we might as well get... a little familiar, y'know?"

There was a murmur of agreement throughout the group, and they then died down once more, and all eyes fell upon the one with the headband.

"Right," he cleared his throat. "I'm Tony. Tony Apollo."

The collective eyes of the group scattered around until the next person spoke. Eventually the guy who first spoke opened his mouth again.

"I'm Griffin Gorr," he said as he crossed his arms and looked away, annoyedly.

"Piper Westley," The orange haired girl said. Tony nodded to her and Griffin as a silent 'thank you,' and joined everyone else in looking for the next person to speak out.

Eventually, another girl called out. This one was taller than Tony and Piper, but shorter than Griffin. Her brown hair was pulled back into a tight ponytail. She looked exceedingly muscular. "Nori Warukata," she said bluntly, and looked away.

Polvo stared at the other four. He was the last one. "Polvo Poplip," he said as he looked at his feet. Looking up, he saw the whole group staring at him.

"Like... Polvo Poplip as in *Travis* Poplip? Ex-CFO of GoroCo?" Tony asked, a little hesitantly.

Polvo sighed. "Yeah. That one."

"What happened between Gorov and your dad?"

"Prefer not to say."

"Ah.. I understand..."

Another silence dawned on the group. Griffin

eventually broke it once more. "Welp. I'm going home," he said as he started walking to the elevator. He pressed the button as the rest of them caught up.

There wasn't much conversation between the group as they eventually reached the first floor, and dispersed in different directions.

"**N**EZUMI," **THE SEWERS MEMBER** smiled as he raised his glass of wine. "To our success."

Nezumi stood with a smile on his face. He clinked glasses and took a sip of the thick, maroon liquid. "Don't drink it all too fast, we only have a little left, don't we?"

The man in the rat mask frowned for a moment, but smiled again. "Perhaps we should... *acquire...* more, hm?"

"Nope," Nezumi quickly said. "Remember the ideals, man. We steal when we *need* to. The desire to celebrate is not a necessity. Just be sparing with the wine, and share."

"But sir, this is an event to celebrate!"

"And celebrate we will! But the ideas Filthus left us with will not die out. Not at least while I'm the King."

The Rat bowed his head, and walked away. Nezumi

sipped his wine once more, and passed it off to another one of the rats walking around. He looked out upon the crowd in front of him, and smiled. He thought to himself for a moment. *If only you could have seen this, Filthus. If only.*

His train of thought was interrupted when another member of the gang walked to him. "Congratulations on another successful raid, sir!"

"Ah," Nezumi put his hands up. "It's all thanks to our numbers. Not everyone can do these things alone."

The Rat shook Nezumi's hand, and proceeded on with the festivities. Nezumi scanned the crowd once more, nodded to himself, and walked into his room. The Sewers' base didn't have many rooms, but the largest was dedicated to the king. The entire place of operations was held underneath the ground, within the massive sewer system of the Surface City.

Inside his quarters, he found another Rat member. This one wearing a few more shiny things than the others.

"Ah, my advisor," Nezumi said as he walked through the room of riches and sat atop a torn leather chair. "I hope I didn't keep you waiting long."

"No worries, sir," The advisor said with a little bow, "None at all."

"Good. What's on your mind? What'cha got for me?"

The advisor dove his hand into his pocket and unveiled a scrap of paper. On it, Nezumi saw the list of factories. The advisor took out a battered pen, and etched a line through one of the buildings towards the bottom of the list. There were still many more on the list.

"Under the reign of Filthus," he started, as he used his pen as a pointer on the paper. "We destroyed nine factories." He pointed to the first nine on the list, all of which had lines through them. Moving the pen downward, he gestured at the factories that had newer lines through them. "Under your reign so far, we've taken down just four."

Nezumi paused for a while. The advisor began sweating nervously. "What exactly are you advising here, advisor?"

"W-Well," the rat stammered. "I'm suggesting we… take down more… I suppose…"

Nezumi made a large gesture with his arms in the air. "Ah, yes!" He shouted sarcastically. "We just gotta take down more factories! Just like that! MAN, How could I have not thought of that myself!?"

The advisor's face burned red underneath his respirator.

"Listen, advisor," Nezumi said, leaning forward in his chair. "For one, I'm not Filthus. I could never even come close to Filthus. He was a greater leader than the Sewers will ever have again. He was one of a kind in Arkoma. And for two, these factories are FAR from as easy as they were when Filthus was around. They've upped the securities tenfold, and that's on a *good* day. I don't know what use they still have for them if they're escaping into the Undercity, but they're sturdier. More heavily guarded."

"I understand, sir," the advisor's voice faltered a bit, before he cleared his throat. "Maybe we could put together somewhat of a reconnaissance team?"

Nezumi leaned forward in his chair again. "...Go on."

"Like... a team of Rats to infiltrate a factory, but instead of destroying it... we just lie low, and gather information on what they're doing with them!"

Nezumi was stunned. It took him a long while before talking again. "Advisor... I think that was the best advisement you've given me in this reign."

"Thank you sir..."

"No, no. Thank *you*."

10

POLVO WASN'T THE FIRST to meet at the main gate. He had woken up a little earlier than usual, due to his stress-induced nightmare, but he elected to stay in bed for as long as possible. Once he gained the gall to roll out from under the covers, he got dressed, and left his house before his parents had the opportunity to say a word. Polvo's father looked down at his feet, ashamed of himself.

Upon arriving at the gate, he found Piper and Nori, standing in an awkward silence. Piper looked relieved to see him.

"Polvo!" She said as she walked up to shake his hand. "Good morning!"

Polvo stretched his hand out to meet hers in the middle, and they shook. Polvo looked to Nori and they hesitantly exchanged their "good morning"s.

A silence dawned upon the three of them for a while,

before being interrupted by Griffin, who walked with a duffle bag slung over his shoulder. It rattled slightly as he walked. He didn't say anything. He looked like he had never woken up this early in his life.

The awkward silence ensued.

Until it was broken, around five minutes later, by the heavily panting Tony. He ran up to the group, totally out of breath.

"Oh… man… I knew… I was gonna be the last one… Sorry guys…" He said as he planted his hands on his knees and hunched over as he breathed. The group exchanged smiles at Tony's expense, and they all felt a little more at ease.

Moments after Tony arrived, Don Gorov emerged from an alleyway near them.

"Alright, you better remember everything that was said last night, 'cause I ain't saying it again. And I don't expect another line of introductions. If you don't remember someone's name, tough it out until someone else says it."

The group looked at each other, each member second guessing themselves on everyone's names.

"Anyways," Don Gorov continued. "Make sure you all got respirators, 'cause the air up there is rapidly declining."

Polvo briefly thought of Dorothy.

"Okay. I hope you brought the weapons, Mr. Gorr," Don Gorov motioned to Griffin's duffle bag and smirked. "Remember to make a scene. Your entrance as the Tempest has gotta be *explosive*. Let Arkoma know who the hell they're dealing with now. Steal from shops, kill some homeless, you get the idea."

Most of the group looked uneasy, but all eventually nodded.

"Right. Let's get this door open, and you guys on your way. Enjoy your time up there. Make me proud. And don't forget to keep close watch on my factories."

The massive gate to the surface remained locked shut, but a small door on the side opened for the group, and they funneled through. It was a bit of a walk to make it all the way to the top, and by the time they made it, Tony was out of breath again.

They all put on their respirators, and stopped before reaching the very top. Griffin slipped the duffle bag from his shoulder and unipped it. The group stared at the assortment of weaponry on display.

"Take what you want," Griffin said as he reached down and grabbed an oversized metallic bat.

Nori grabbed an old looking ball-and-chain style flail. Piper grabbed three daggers.

Tony smiled, and grabbed an ornate looking pair of gauntlets.

And Polvo grabbed a sword, one that had somewhat of a hook on the end of it.

The group sat there for a moment and tested out their various weapons. They all seemed pretty satisfied.

"Alright," Griffin broke the silence. "Let's go."

He strode forward, closely followed by Nori. The remaining three took a collected deep breath, and trudged after them.

Piercing through to the surface, the group stood for a moment, looking around.The city hadn't changed much, most of them noted, but Polvo knew how much was different. He knew the people. They looked a bit more down. A bit more unhealthy. A bit more vulnerable.

"So…" Tony said. "What should we do to start..?"

Griffin looked annoyed. He marched through the street, up to a homeless man, begging for spare coin. The man looked up at him, and rattled his can of money.

"Give it to me," Griffin said, without emotion. The man looked confused, and eventually angry. Griffin adjusted his bat on his shoulder, and the man grew afraid. But fear wasn't enough. Griffin swiped the can from the man's hands, sending what little money he'd collected across the street. The man's confusion grew stronger.

"Why..?" He asked weakly. He didn't have a respirator. Griffin smirked, and un-shouldered his bat. One clean swing to the stomach crumpled the beggar. Polvo looked on in horror.

Griffin kneeled down to the man, gasping for breath. "Tell all your pathetic fucking friends that we're the Tempest. We rob for *fun,* and we kill for *pleasure.* Now go. Get the fuck out of our sight."

The man sobbed as he scrambled to his feet, and limped away. Piper and Tony exchanged their fair shares of mortified expressions from under their respirators. Polvo looked horrified. Nori stood, unaffected.

Griffin walked back to the group, panting slightly. He looked among the rest of the group. "So, are Nori, Polvo, and I gonna have to do all the heavy lifting here or something?"

Tony and Piper looked at Polvo. They couldn't see his expression from under his respirator, since it covered his whole face. Griffin nodded to Polvo and Nori and started walking away. Nori followed immediately. Polvo stood there for a moment, wondering whether or not to say something to Piper and Tony. He knew what Don Gorov could do to his family if he disappointed him.

Polvo bit the inside of his cheek, and turned to walk with Griffin and Nori.

Piper and Tony eventually followed.

———⟫◆⟪———

Polvo stood awkwardly on the street corner. The group decided to split up for a few hours, so they can broaden their influence. Polvo made sure to keep the group as far away from Dorothy's shop as possible.

Dorothy.

What Polvo would give to see her right now.

He thought to himself for a moment, and decided *'To hell with the Tempest for a bit,'* and began walking to the Economy Hub.

As he walked, he hoped that Nori or Griffin hadn't wandered there. She had it rough enough living on the surface.

Eventually nearing the shop, he paused from afar, and looked around the area to make sure it was clear. It seemed that way enough. He walked in.

Behind the counter, where Dorothy's mother usually stood, stood Dorothy. She looked bored. Polvo approached the counter, and peeled his respirator off his face. A few breaths of bad air wouldn't kill him. He needed to see her with nothing but his eyes.

Dorothy looked up, and saw him. A smile split across her face, and she practically jumped over the counter, embracing him in a hug. They sat there, holding each other for a moment, before pulling away, and locking lips.

After that, Polvo slipped his respirator back on. It was only then, when he realised that Dorothy wasn't wearing one.

"Where's your respirator?"

She paused for a while. "I needed to sell it," she said, dodging his eye contact.

"What!? Why?"

Another pause, but this one ended with tears streaking her face. She went on to explain the financial hardship that had come upon her shop, and eventually she wept as she revealed the death of her mother.

Polvo held her. They shed tears together. And as they sat together, Polvo realized something he thought he needed to do. He stood, and told Dorothy that he needed to leave. She lifted his respirator and gave him another kiss, before returning behind the counter. Polvo waved goodbye, and exited the shop. He knew what he needed to do. He knew he had to join Griffin and Nori.

⬤◆⬤

Polvo wandered for a while, before eventually spotting one of his group members. It was Nori. He thought about it for a while before deciding to approach her.

"How are things going over here?"

Nori looked at him, and pulled a bag off of her back. Unzipping it, she showed Polvo the various items and money she had mugged from people.

"Ah... Nice," Polvo said hesitantly. He had no idea what to think of her. She really didn't give anything to work with conversationally. He decided he'd try anyway.

"So, what's your story? How'd Gorov get you into his mitts?"

Nori stared at him for a minute, but eventually opened her mouth to speak. "My father," she started. "He was a criminal on the surface, but he was eventually hired by Don Gorov. Behind his back though, my father still continued his life of crime, and eventually was arrested by Gorov himself. He's holding him along with my mother in prison in the Undercity. I'm basically working for him to lessen my family's sentences."

"Fuck..."

"Yeah."

They stood there for a while in silence.

"I'm sorry," Polvo started, and reached a hand

towards her shoulder. SHe pulled away before he had the chance to make contact.

"Don't," she snapped. "Being upset and sad about it won't change anything. I just have to do the work I'm given. That's all."

Polvo was going to apologize again, but she had already started walking away. He followed her down an alleyway, where they found another homeless man. They briefly looked at each other, and both took their first step towards him.

11

TRAVIS POPLIP SEEMED TO scare himself awake. He sat up in his bed, panting and sweating. He looked to his still-sleeping wife beside him, and he breathed a little sigh of relief. A little silver lining to his situation. He pulled the covers from himself and planted his feet on the ground. He stood, and silently walked to his study.

Pushing the door open and closing it behind him, he sighed once more and tried his best to blink the oncoming tears from his eyes. He opened the study door again, and peeked into Polvo's empty room. It was then, when he couldn't blink the tears away anymore. Closing the study door behind him again, he wept softly as he walked to his desk. He sat down and pulled a leather-bound journal from one of the desk drawers.

Flipping through the pages, he continued to cry as he overlooked his old plans. He looked through the window in the wall and stared at the GoroCo tower. He trembled with anger. After a few beats, he snapped the journal shut, and tucked it into the chest pocket of his jacket that still hung from the rack. Grabbing a nearby sheet of paper, he clicked the cap off a pen, and began scribbling a letter. He tried his best not to drip his own tears onto the paper.

Eventually signing his name at the bottom, he took a deep breath in through his running nose, and sighed as he sealed the letter in an envelope, and left it on the surface of his desk. Standing from his chair, he grabbed his coat, and walked out the door. He locked the front door behind him, and started towards GoroCo tower.

——◆◇◆——

Don Gorov looked at scraps of paper that had been laid upon his desk. Each little scrap had around a paragraph written on it. He scanned a few of them, before looking up impatiently at the man who laid them on his desk. The man shifted his footing uncomfortably.

"You clutter my desk, when you could've just told me out loud what was happening up there?"

"I-I'm sorry sir," he stammered. "I thought you'd want to see the reports firsthand. I'd be more than happy to give you the synopsis," he said as he scrambled forward and grabbed at the parchments. Don Gorov furrowed his brow and rubbed the bridge of his nose.

"Alright..," he started as he read through the pieces. "It seems Griffin Gorr made the first move once they got to the surface, attacking a homeless beggar, and scattering his money through the street..." Don Gorov stopped his disappointed behavior and cracked a smile.

"Then, it seems they split up after that...," he flipped through a few more. "But Piper Westley and Tony Apollo stayed together. Nori Warukatta and Polvo Poplip went on their own..."

"Tell me what Polvo did," Don Gorov said suddenly. The man blinked a few times, and started sifting through the pieces of paper again.

"Uhh... Polvo... went into the Economy Hub... and... went into the Vorgund shop for around... and hour maybe? He left empty handed."

Don Gorov gritted his teeth. He was about to snap at the man, but his train of thought was interrupted by the man's continuation.

"It seems that after leaving the shop, he met up with Miss Warukatta, and... oh... dear," the man swallowed uncomfortably.

"Well?" Don Gorov said impatiently.

Before the man continued, there was a loud knock

on the door. Don Gorov sighed, and motioned for the man to leave. "We'll continue this later."

The man nodded, and hurried out of the room. When he opened the door, Don Gorov got a glance of Travis Poplip before he entered. He didn't look happy.

"Travis," Don Gorov said as he looked to a clock on his desk. "A bit late for you, isn't it?"

"I want my son out of the Tempest," Travis said as he approached the massive desk, and aggressively placed his hands upon it.

"Straight to business then," Don Gorov said as he nonchalantly leaned back in his chair and laced his fingers behind his head.

"I'm serious Gorov. Let him out. I don't care what you do to me... But let him out."

"How sentimental... But what's in it for me? It sounds like I'd be losing a crucial member to the team, and getting really nothing from it... You and I both know your days on the surface are over. Arkoma chewed you up, and spat you back out."

Travis laughed. "You say that as though you weren't on your knees right there with me."

Don Gorov's expression darkened. "I don't like you coming into my office, telling me what to do, Travis."

"I remember when you used to call it *our* office, you fucking bastard."

Don Gorov slammed his fists on the desk and shot up from his chair. "For that, I should have your fucking *head* on a *pike*. Get out of my office. *Now.*"

"Let. Polvo. Go."

The two stared at each other for a long time. Neither one backing down. The air was palpable.

Travis suddenly pulled the journal from his coat pocket. Don Gorov's eyes darted to it, and for just a moment, he lost his composure.

"Yeah, that's right. You know *exactly* what this is. I could fucking *ruin* you. *So easily.*"

Don Gorov sat back down, and put his hands underneath his desk. Silently, he began fondling through the various drawers.

"Alright then. Let's take this a bit easier," he said as he wrapped his hand around a familiar handle. Slipping the item into his coat pocket, he rose once more. "Travis, think about how much we've been through. After all this, and after all I've done for you, you'd do this? Ruining me would leave you dead in the water."

Travis' expression faltered.

Don Gorov smiled.

Approaching him, Don Gorov outstretched his hands. "C'mon, buddy. We can work around this."

"Polvo doesn't know how much I've done for him. And how much I love him. I've fucked up so much in life, and I don't want Polvo making the same decisions I did before. I want him to have a normal life in this fucked up world… I want him to be better than I ever was."

Don Gorov took another step forward. "I understand. And that's really touching… Believe me… I'd want my son to be better than me as well…"

Travis bowed his head as Don Gorov got even closer. The pain he felt in his heart was overbearing.

It made the pain of the knife entering his abdomen almost feel good.

Don Gorov belted out a laugh as he kicked Travis' legs out from under him. Travis hit the ground, coughing and sputtering. He looked down at the handle of his old hunting knife, and at his own blood, soaking his shirt around the entrypoint.

"Come *on*, Travis," Don Gorov started pacing as he bellowed into the air. "You *really* think the people of this city would give *half a shit* how I got where I am today? The world is *over*. The planet is *dead*. But *we* are alive. That, my friend, is what matters to people. We're alive, and we're gonna *stay* alive. How? That doesn't matter. All these people know is that GoroCo is currently burying the last of humanity in the ground, where we'll continue living for *centuries*. You think leaking my *dirty laundry* will make these people change *any ounce* of their support for me?"

Travis couldn't choke words out of his mouth. The blood he coughed from his throat would be replaced by more just a moment later.

"I thought you were a little slow to the uptake sometimes, but *come on*. These people don't care about *me*. They care about the fact that they are *alive*."

"*p...po...*" Travis gagged.

Don Gorov stopped his pacing, and walked back to Travis. He knelt down and looked his old comrade in the eyes. He watched casually as the color drained from Travis' face.

"*Polvo..,*" he managed, before collapsing onto his back. Don Gorov watched as the blood slowly filled his gaped mouth, before beginning to spill down his cheeks. Any ounce of regret Don Gorov felt was brushed away with a sigh, as he walked back to his desk and sat in his chair. He clapped his huge hands, and a couple workers walked through the massive doors, and grabbed Travis' motionless body.

"That's right, old buddy," he said to himself under his breath.

"Polvo."

12

POLVO'S MIND WANDERED AS he slowly walked through the Surface City. Blocking everything he had done from his memory, he trudged along towards the entrance to the Undercity. *Was this really his life now? Did he have to just come up here and hurt people for the rest of his working years?* He was far from pleased at the idea.

Eventually he made it to the entrance. He hadn't known if the other members of the Tempest had made it back yet, and for the most part, he didn't care. He just wanted to lie down in bed, and let his brain turn off for a while. He started down the path, and let his mind wander again.

Eventually passing through all the security, he peeled off his respirator, and started the trek home. He looked along the Undercity streets, and watched the children of rich parents, playing amongst themselves.

He watched their smiles. He remembered smiling like that once with Dorothy.

Fuck.

He wanted to find a way to get Dorothy down there. He needed to keep her safe. Without her, there wasn't anything in the world for him.

He made it to his house. He opened the front door and meandered up the stairs to his room. Collapsing into his bed, he was practically asleep as soon as he hit the pillow.

———◆———

Polvo jolted awake in his bed. He shivered as he wanted to forget the dream that had awoken him. Seeing that old man again. Seeing Griffin. He layed back down and rolled over, wanting to sleep peacefully again. He tossed and turned for a while, before ultimately giving up, and stepping out of bed. Pulling some clothes over himself, he turned towards his door, and walked through.

Polvo peeked into his parents room, and saw only one figure under the covers. *Dad must be out drinking again or something,* he thought as he silently said goodbye, and snuck through the front door.

The streets of the Undercity were quiet at night. Normally, there were guards patrolling the residential areas, but hey, nobody's perfect. Especially if you get paid an unreasonable amount of money to watch over a city of people that don't need to commit crimes.

Skulking along the sidewalks, Polvo followed his natural route to his secret door to the surface. Upon reaching it though, the door looked different. The makeshift lever he had crafted seemed to have been removed in not the nicest kind of ways. He frowned, and looked around the dark alleyway for another item to use to get the door open.

Suddenly, a voice. An all-too recognizable voice.

"Holy *hell*, kiddo," Don Gorov called out as he emerged at the entrance to the alleyway. "Let me know when you plan on taking so fucking long to try to get back up there. Guys had to keep me awake for hours."

"What do you want, Gorov?" Polvo asked as he continued eying the ground, but rather for a makeshift lever, moreso a makeshift weapon.

"Originally, I was gonna deliver this whole intimidating speech thing, but I'm far too tired for that now. I'll give it to ya straight. No more goin' up there for ya. Not without my okay. You're workin' for me now, and that means I own you. And I say 'no more secret door.'"

Polvo gritted his teeth as he stared at Gorov. There was a palpable silence for a moment, before Don Gorov started pacing back and forth. "Been a busy night for me, y'know," he said as he stared upwards and watched his breath in the cold night. "Had to do something I didn't want to do. Didn't think I'd have to," he said, showing a surprising amount of emotion. Polvo stared daggers at him, trying to decipher what he meant. He had a couple ideas, but none that he wanted to give any more thought. He gave up the idea of intimidating the massive man in front of him, and started the uncomfortably long walk out of the alleyway. As he passed Gorov, the man gave him a large pat on the shoulder. "Rest up. Another big day up there tomorrow," he said with a sneer.

Polvo said nothing, and kept walking. He didn't know how, but he'd find a way up to her again. Gorov would have to kill him to make him stop. But how could he do it?

His train of thought was broken by a familiar set of footsteps. Light, almost dainty, but determined. Polvo turned around and looked down at Piper. Her curly red hair was tied up into a giant puff-ball behind her head. The street lights glistened off the lenses of her round glasses.

"How long have you been-"

"Long enough. Come on, I have an idea," she said as she grabbed Polvo's wrist, and pulled him along the dimly lit sidewalk.

"Where are we-"

"Near my place, there's kind of a thin spot. My family and I live close to the wall, so we're relatively close to the Surface."

Polvo fell silent as he understood, and they continued walking.

"It's a girl, right?" Piper broke the silence between them.

Polvo paused for a little. "Yeah," he eventually sighed. "Been friends since we were little, then my family got approved to move down here. I'm not ready to let her go."

"I understand. I had a similar situation, actually…"

Polvo looked down at her. "Well, if there's anyone that would understand your feelings, it's me. I can listen, if you want to talk."

Piper hesitated, but eventually sighed. "I have someone up there too. That's… actually why I'm in the Tempest. My dad knows Don Gorov through work. He's an engineer. When I said I didn't want to be a part of the gang, Don Gorov threatened me with hurting her, and I had to join. I know he doesn't want me seeing her, but at least I know she'll be as safe as she can be up there."

"Fuck," Polvo grimaced. "I fucking hate him."

Piper choked back tears and silently nodded.

The moment was halted as the two stopped in front of an alleyway.

"We should be right under the Economy Hub, actually," Piper said as she walked into the darkness. Polvo quickly followed her in, and they eventually reached the dead end. A rusted pickaxe sat beside the makeshift entrance. Polvo peered into the improvised walkway.

"You were already digging?"

"Yeah," Piper said as she grabbed the pick and started walking up. "You're not the only one that wanted to see their girl."

Polvo smiled and walked in after her.

13

"**A**LRIGHT PEOPLE, ANOTHER DAY,** another dollar. Let's do good up there huh?" Don Gorov said enthusiastically to the Tempest members. He was responded to with silence as the group trudged up to the gates of the Surface City. Griffin and Nori exchanged a brief glance. As did Polvo and Piper. Tony stared at the ground and yawned as he walked.

"Still hate how early we gotta do this," Tony mumbled mid-way through another yawn. "'Specially if we have to like… beat people up and shit."

The rest of them shared a collective eye roll, and they continued their solemn march. As they neared the top, they stretched their muscles a bit, and readied their respirators. They broke the seal to the gate, and cracked it open just far enough for Griffin to stick his head out. Making sure the coast was clear, they pushed the door open enough for them all to slip through, and quickly shut it behind them. Don Gorov had made sure to tell them how important it was that no one saw them coming in and out of the Undercity, for obvious reasons.

"Well," Polvo said absentmindedly as he started to walk away. "Suppose we should split up again, huh? Cover more ground? Like last time? Yeah, alrighty."

"Stop," Nori spoke sharply, and Polvo froze mid-stride. "We should stick together today. We hardly created any impact last time. We need to establish ourselves."

Tony scanned through the group with his eyes. "And how might we do that?"

Nori looked to Griffin and they shared another glance.

"I guess we'll see," Nori said as she started walking. Griffin followed immediately, but Polvo, Piper, and Tony hesitated for a moment before meandering along.

As the group traced along the sidewalks of the city, bystanders started to grow in numbers. They neared one of the main districts of the inner city, locally dubbed the Center City. Here, the vast majority of gang violence and basic integration occurred. The Surface City of Arkoma was home to many gangs, with the oldest being the Sewers. Other examples included the Scavengers, the Tinkerers, the Ocean, the Hunters

Guild, and more; each with their respective territories and colorful members.

And now, it was time for the Tempest to join that list.

As they walked along, Nori and Griffin eyed passersby like hawks. The rest of the group seemed to just eye the two in front of them.

Suddenly, as the group reached one of the main streets, Nori lunged out and grabbed someone. A frail looking older man. No respirator. As soon as she did this, Griffin followed suit, with a younger looking, but probably just as weak, young man. The old man seemed to crumble into Nori's grasp, but the younger man made a yelp, and struggled under the strength of Griffin. The other three stood frozen. The passersby mistook their frozen fear for stoic complacence.

"*LOOK HERE*," Griffin screamed into the crowd. The people on the streets of Arkoma didn't usually take heed to people screaming in public, but the boom behind Griffin's voice definitely made its impact. Many people stopped and turned to the cause of the noise. Almost in perfect unison, Griffin and Nori brandished knives, and held them high in the air. "*FEAR THE*

TEMPEST," Griffin boomed once more, as the two dropped their arms, and executed the people.

There was a collected gasp among the crowd, and most people started to move away. Griffin and Nori kicked the bodies into the road, but stood above them for a while longer. Polvo stared into the crowd. The fear in people's eyes. It was something that could never escape them. Polvo's train of thought was broken as someone pierced through the crowd. The respirator they dawned resembled the head of a rat. This person was a member of the Sewers.

"What did they do to you's guys? Huh? What's the deal?!"

Griffin didn't have anything to say. He caught himself thinking about the question a bit too long. Nori broke the silence with a single word. *"Territory."* The Sewers member cocked his head to the side. "Territory? Really? The main square of the Center City is your territory?"

"Arkoma is our territory," Tony said from behind. Griffin and Nori smiled under their respirators. Piper and Polvo uneasily looked at Tony. The member of the Sewers looked around at the disappearing crowd.

"Yeah, we'll see about that one," he said as he disappeared into the masses.

Polvo stared hard at Griffin and Nori. He knew

they would be an issue from the start, but this was unbelievable. He hesitantly looked at the bodies on the ground. He knew he had created a life of petty crime for himself, but this was beyond anything he could've imagined. These were people. Real people. One old, one younger. And the people he's supposed to call his crewmates just murdered them in the street for no reason. Polvo definitely didn't appreciate that.

"Alright, you've made your scene," Piper broke the tense silence. "Come on Polvo, let's go," she said sternly while she grabbed Polvo's arm and pulled him away. Through the glint in her round glasses, Polvo could see the tears welling in her red face.

———◆———

"I can't believe it…" Dorothy trailed off as she looked across the table at Polvo and Piper. "This is all just… too much…" she said uncomfortably as she broke eye contact and stared down at the ground.

"Hey," Polvo said as he reached across the table and grabbed her hands. "I'll be okay, alright? I'm gonna figure a way out of this. I won't hurt anyone."

"I know *you* won't hurt anyone, but who's gonna hurt *you*?" She asked, tears streaking down her face.

"Piper," Polvo said as he looked at her.

"Right, I understand. I'll see you later, Polvo," Piper nodded and walked out of the shop.

"Hey, hey. I'm here Dorothy. I'm here."

"Why can't it stay like that then?" She said, finally looking back up at him. That sent Polvo over the edge. Tears of his own streaming down. He stood from the table and walked around to her side. Helping her stand from her chair, they locked lips. The two stood there for a moment, in that position, and as they separated, they looked into each other's eyes, before mutually leaning in once more. They cried together.

14

POLVO TRUDGED HOME FROM the Vorgund shop. He sighed, and stared up into the unmoving clouds of smoke that blocked out the stars. Polvo recalled once before being able to see through the smoke, at the right time of day. Those days were long gone though.

He wished he could stay. He wished with all his heart, he'd never have to go into the Undercity again. He wished he could stay with Dorothy, and start a family, amidst the horrible world they lived in. She made him happy. It was always her.

Passing through the door to the Undercity, he checked the board nailed to the wall. Listed on it were the names of all the members of the Tempest. All the names had a little mark beneath them, except for Polvo. As he walked by, he etched a mark underneath it, and sealed the door behind him. There were three massive deadbolts that locked the door, and Don Gorov instructed that the last member inside was to lock the door. Polvo had always wondered what would happen if he were to just leave the door wide open.

He thought about that as he walked home. As his train of thought continued to chug along, he thought of his dad. Where had he been? He was more than usually in his office reading, or eating something in the kitchen by the time Polvo had left. He figured he'd find his dad waiting for him when he got home.

Polvo's thought train seemed to stop at the station when he started thinking of his dad. He moved onto just thinking about his parents in general. They had raised him to be a model citizen, and a worthy resident of the Undercity, but he never really felt as though he deserved it. Born into the world of the rich, but being raised alongside the poor. He felt caught in between. A social class of his own, where no one else fit into. Somewhere where he didn't belong, no matter how hard he tried to fit in.

Eventually he reached his house. He walked through the front door, and checked the kitchen for his dad. Nothing. Probably the office then. He marched up the stairs, and into his office. Empty.

Polvo noticed a letter in the center of the desk. He looked around the office nervously as he took the first few steps in. As he neared the desk, he noticed the slightly yellowed envelope was addressed to him. He cocked his head to the side, and reached out for it. Tearing it open, he read to himself.

Polvo;

I know things between us haven't been the best throughout your lifetime. But believe me when I say this; I love you more than anything else in this twisted world. And from the bottom of my heart, I'm sorry. I could never apologize enough to satisfy the sins I've committed in this life of mine. It eats away at me at night knowing I have a gift like you, after everything else I've done. It feels wrong to be rewarded for doing so many unspeakable things.

And now I fear the blood that drenches my hands has begun to drip itself unto yours.

Don Gorov is far from the man he says he is. I know you know that though. It pains me to say this, but the Tempest project you find yourself in now, was my idea. Back before you, before your mother, before everything, I had Gorov. We were like brothers. Inseparable. We laughed together, we lived together... We killed together.

The Tempest was an idea created as soon as we established GoroCo. A way of defense in the form of a gang. In theory, it was perfect. Allowing us to keep things in order from a business standpoint, and to have guaranteed eyes and ears among the people. It was perfect... And now Gorov has done what we agreed never to do.

Polvo I know I said it before but I love you. I'm unsure if you'll ever hear from me again, but please, just know, despite everything I've done in my life, I'd do it all over again if it meant I got to spend another lifetime with you. You're my son. My only son. And I'm so proud of you. I'm so proud of the man you've become. I'm sorry I won't be able to see how your story ends. I fear I'm rapidly approaching the end of mine. And part of me hopes you'll never have to see it.

I love you Polvo. And I'm sorry,
Dad

Polvo's hands shook as he finished the letter. The tears that flushed into his eyelids strained against the barriers, and eventually won as he blinked. Tears streamed down his face as he quietly wept. He gripped the letter to his chest, and let his knees give out. Bowing his head to the floor of his father's study, he clutched the last words as he sobbed into the carpet. He had lived so long resenting his parents, unknowingly thinking they felt anywhere close to similarly as him. The newfound love from his father felt nothing but bitter. It wasn't fair. Why was his father allowed to confess love, and he couldn't do the same?

Polvo spent the night in the study that night, after eventually passing out.

15

T WAS A QUIET evening at the Sewers' home base. The occasional water drips echoed throughout the intricate tunnels of the Arkoman sewer system. Nezumi sat in his chambers, idly fiddling with a couple rocks and bones. His doors suddenly opened. He looked up at the Rat mask walking towards him without moving his head.

"Sir, I have something to report," the Rat uncomfortably spoke as he rubbed his hands together.

"Report away then," Nezumi said, adjusting his position in his throne-like chair.

"It seems as though there's... a new gang in the city..."

Nezumi's eyebrows actually twitched upwards. He sat forward in his chair. "Out with it then, what is it?"

The Rat frantically pulled out a slip of paper and read from it. "They call themselves The Tempest... and they killed two innocents in the Center City square today… One of ours asked them why they did it, and they claimed that the two were in their territory. They went on to exclaim that all of Arkoma was their territory…"

Nezumi leaned forward and sat his elbows on his knees as he interlaced his fingers in front of his mouth. "Okay. Thank you. Is there anything else?"

"Not that I can think of, sir."

"You may go then. Thanks again."

"Right then sir. Looking forward to another successful outing tomorrow," the Rat said as he bowed, and exited the chambers.

Nezumi breathed a heavy sigh. He grabbed his pen and stared at the papers in front of him on the surface of his desk. The plans detailed another raid on a factory. Various scribbles accompanied the structure, showing guard stations, and other finer details. Towards the top corner of the plans, he scribbled something, and set the pen down. He stood up from his chair and started pacing around the room. Eventually stopping in his tracks, he looked back at what he scribbled.

The Tempest..?

16

POLVO WAS WOKEN BY pounding on his door. His head shot up, and the first sensation he felt was the pain in his back from sleeping on the floor of his father's office. The pounding on the door continued, and Polvo let himself collapse to the ground again. He listened as his mother hastily got out of bed, and walked past him, down the stairs, and opened the door. He tried to recognize the voice that started talking through the grogginess in his brain. He found his feet beneath him, and already rushing down the stairs by the time he realized it was Griffin's voice. First it was his father. He wouldn't let his mother share a similar fate, especially at the hands of someone to be considered his comrade. He wiped the crusted tears from his cheeks, and immediately stood in front of his mother.

"What is it, Griffin?" He said, trying not to sound as stern as he did.

"Fuck, Polvo, not much sleep or something?" He replied, taken slightly aback. "Whatever," he said as he shook his head. "Boss has an emergency task for us. We need to leave now."

Polvo cursed under his breath, and told Griffin to give him a minute. Closing the door, he gave his mother a massive embrace. He didn't have the time it would've taken to explain everything going on. He didn't think he ever would. He wondered if that amount of time even existed. Holding back new tears, he rushed back up the stairs, and grabbed his father's letter from the office floor. He clutched it tightly to his chest once more, before neatly folding it back into the envelope, and pushing it into his inside coat pocket.

Polvo didn't have much to prepare, considering he slept in all his clothes the night before. Pushing himself down the stairs once more, he gave his mother another hug, and walked out to meet Griffin again.

"What happened? What're we doing?"

"Apparently the Sewers are taking on another factory today. We found out late last night. Gorov wants us to go up there and fight."

"Fuck," Polvo said under his breath.

"Yeah, pretty much," Griffin said as the two marched towards the gate to the surface.

Upon their arrival, Polvo realized they were the last

ones there. Piper and Tony looked admittedly terrible. Extremely tired, and not in the best fighting condition. Nori looked uneasily normal. As Griffin and Polvo approached, Don Gorov emerged from the shadows of the gate.

"Right. I'm sure Griffin gave you the rundown on what you guys will be doing today, if he didn't ask him on the way. I'm not explaining it again."

The group nodded, and Don Gorov gestured towards the gate. He watched them start up the ramp. Polvo looked over his shoulder at the massive man and stared daggers into him. Don Gorov returned the look with an inquisitive stare. Head cocked to the side, it was almost as if Polvo could hear him thinking *'Do you know what I did?'*

The Tempest continued to trudge up the ramp, and Don Gorov turned away from Polvo's gaze. As they disappeared up the ramp, Polvo watched as he walked away. He couldn't shake the rage inside him. It scared him more than anything else. As the group neared the top of the gate, they propped the door open a little, checked to see if anyone was watching, and eventually darted out in the direction of the factory.

<hr>

Nezumi woke up in his massive makeshift mattress, covered in his massive makeshift blanket. Only the best garbage and scraps for the Rat King. He could her the main chamber of the Sewers base from his room. The bustling and hustling of the Sewers members as they prepared for another attempted takedown of a factory. Nezumi listened to the whitenoise for a while, before pulling himself from his nest. Pulling his clothes on, he let out a loud, raspy cough before securing his respirator onto his head. Most people in the Sewers slept with the respirator on, but Nezumi desired no such discomfort, even at the expense of his own lungs. He figured he wouldn't live long enough to see the ill effects anyways.

As he exited his bed, he trudged over to his desk. Scanning over the plans he had scanned over so many times now, he found that his eyes got caught on the newest addition. *The Tempest..?*

He froze for a moment and thought about it, but eventually shrugged the thought from his mind, and continued readying himself for the big day. Eventually, he pushed his door open, and was immediately greeted by the army of Rats. He chuckled at the enthusiasm. Despite the unreasonable danger and mortality rate of these raids, it truly seemed that the members of the Sewers looked forward to nothing more.

"Alright, people!" He bellowed into the crowd. "Let's get another one under our belts today!"

———◆———

As the Tempest got into position around the factory, Polvo stared upwards at the immense smokestack, billowing thick black soot into the air. "Fuck," he said under his breath. "No wonder these guys destroy these things." His train of thought was eventually interrupted by the distant sounds of footsteps. His eyes darted around the perimeter, where the other members of the group were stationed, spread out from each other to cover more ground. He watched as the rest of their eyes also shot towards the footsteps. All morning, they had heard the sounds of pedestrian foot traffic, but this was something more. This was a horde. This was the Sewers.

Polvo watched the rest of the Tempest ready their weapons. He scoffed to himself and shook his head. Even with the help of the security at the factory, there's no chance in hell they could pull this off.

As the footsteps got louder and louder, a sound ripped through the air. Polvo nearly jumped out of his skin at the sound of metal screaming against itself as the gates to the factory perimeter squealed open.

Looks like Gorov had an army of his own.

Polvo stared in awe as he watched the huge group of armed guards surface from within the factory. He looked up once more, and the smoke still billowed.

As the Sewers came into view, The guards stood at the ready. He noticed some of the members of the guard looked like average citizens of the Surface City. Gorov had paid them to make the Tempest seem bigger. Polvo's eyes were ripped from the guards as he stared at the oncoming gang horde. He noticed in the front, the man leading the march, with an ornate, but obviously handmade, crown atop his respirator. Polvo had heard of him before.

Nezumi, Rat King of the Sewers.

Heir to Filthus.

And before Polvo knew it, they were charging.

Each side bellowed their various battle cries as the Sewers sprinted towards the gates. The guards and the Tempest held their ground, and either shouted back, or gritted their teeth in preparation of what was to come.

Nezumi sprinted, a crude, unpolished sword in his hand raised high. Polvo watched as Griffin readied his metal bat, and jumped from cover. From Griffin, Polvo's eyes jumped to Nori, who had already left cover, and had begun swinging her flail above her head. Then, to Piper. She sat with her daggers in hand, but she still seemed to be crumbled behind her hiding spot. Tony was nearby, his gauntlets lightly rattling with his trembling hands.

Polvo felt his hands sway towards the hilt of his sword, but they hesitated. He took a few heavy deep breaths as the sounds of battle slowly gained volume in his ears, and as the Sewers clashed with the guards, the sounds of all out war boomed. His head pounded from within as he looked up once more from behind cover. Watching Griffin clubbing through multiple people at once with his swings, and Nori almost elegantly juggling through gang members with her flail.

Piper stayed where she was, but Tony had now gotten up, punching at people with all his might. He looked terrified.

Polvo locked eyes with Piper from across the battlefield. She shook her head. He could see the tears in her eyes from there. He shook his head back at her, and slowly grabbed the hilt of his sword.

Jumping out of cover, he stared at the massive conglomeration of people in front of him. The crowd moved hypnotically with the tempo of battle, and it grew ever so slowly smaller in size. Polvo tried to zero in on Nezumi again, but he had lost him within the fight. He realized though, that not every member of the Sewers even had weapons. They were just grappling as best as they could against fully armed opponents. Even the best equipped members had metal pipes, and maybe makeshift armor made from scrap metal.

Polvo decided his course of action. He wouldn't take a single life on this battlefield. He sought to only duel the ones with weapons, and incapacitate them. But doing that with a sword seemed impractical.

Throwing his sword back to his spot of cover, he ran into the crowd. Pushing and punching through people, he eventually landed upon a Rat with a long metal pipe in his hands, Polvo grabbed at it, with no luck. As the rest of the Sewers in the crowd pushed past the two, a small clearing seemed to open for the two duelists. Polvo took another deep breath.

"I don't want to kill you," he yelled over the sounds of screaming and clashing.

"That makes one of us, then," the Rat replied as he lunged forward, and brought the pipe down towards Polvo.

Sidestepping just barely out of the way, Polvo ground his teeth together as he dashed towards the gang member. Before he could ready his pipe again, Polvo's fist collided with his jaw. The Rat's head snapped towards the ground, and his body surged backwards from the blow.

Following through with the punch, Polvo found himself off balance. He watched as the Rat caught himself as he shot his foot behind him, and quickly pointed his head back at Polvo. As Polvo postured again, the Rat pulled his respirator down, and spat out a broken, brown tooth.

Polvo looked down at his newly split knuckles. He shook his head and shook the flashing pain from his wrist as he readied his fist once more.

As the two charged again, Polvo's vision seemed to tunnel in on his opponent. He couldn't see anyone else. He couldn't hear anyone else. He brought his fist to his ear and readied his arm to let loose once more.

He barely had enough time to stop himself as he watched the dagger blade split through the front of the Rat's chest.

DON GOROV TAPPED HIS fingers rhythmically on his desk as he stared at the Tempest members in front of him. They stood, silent. Polvo stared his usual daggers into the businessman, but he hardly seemed to care, if not notice at all.

The ornate wooden desk resonated the sounds of his tapping beautifly. They could hear his foot tapping as well. Eventually, a smile cracked through his face.

"I gotta hand it to you guys," he said, breaking the silence. "Great, great work up there yesterday. Really good stuff, I love to see it."

The Tempest remained silent.

"You saved the factory! And with a staggeringly low loss rate for the good guys!" He said enthusiastically. "That's us, by the way," he chucked.

Polvo didn't blink.

Don Gorov's smile wavered.

"Okay. This is the part when you guys get happy as well, yeah? I don't remember telling you guys to lose your damned *souls* up there huh?"

The Tempest remained silent.

Don Gorov's smile faded all together.

"Okay. *Okay*. So *what if we* lost one? You guys really aren't seeing the bigger picture here. You went up there to risk your necks for my factory, and one of you really went through with it. I see that as a good thing, if anything!"

"How *dare* you," Piper said as the tears under her eyelids spilled out.

Don Gorov grimaced.

"I'm gonna pretend I didn't hear that. And that you only said it because you're so tired from fighting off the human waste that tries to kill my business."

Polvo put his hand on Piper's shoulder.

"Whatever," Don Gorov said. "If you guys refuse to be happy, no skin off my back. I just grabbed you all here first to congratulate you, but that was a shitshow; and second, to tell you we're finishing this fight for real in two days. We know the Sewers backpedaled back to their little home base, but I had a guy following them the whole time. You're gonna go there and finish them off once and for all. Now get out. You're ruining my mood."

Polvo, Piper, Griffin, and Tony exited the office.

POLVO SIGHED AS HE walked through the streets of the Undercity. He limped slightly, courtesy of the battle. Trudging through the same path he had followed nights before, he ended up at the tunnel behind Piper's house. Crawling through, he eventually broke off into the sewer system wall they had dug through. Climbing up the ladder and through the manhole, he turned straight towards Dorothy's shop.

Peeking through the curtains, he scanned the dark room. His eyes landed upon Dorothy, reading a book in the candlelight on the counter. She looked entranced by the book in front of her, as she hardly noticed Polvo walking in. She suddenly reeled to the left and let out a raspy cough, before finally noticing Polvo.

"Polvo!" She gasped as she ran from behind the counter and into his arms.

"Nasty cough coming on, huh?" He looked down

at her through his respirator mask at first, before removing it and interlacing his lips with hers.

"Yeah that's new," she said in between kisses.

"You need a respirator. The air is only going to get worse."

"I know."

A moment of silence dawned as the two halted their romantic antics. It wasn't long before Polvo broke it.

"Dorothy, I love you. I love you more than anyone I've ever met before. The way you make me feel, the way you engage me when we interact. Everything about you just seems to line up so perfectly with me. You're the one I want in my life. You're the one I want to grow old with. To have kids with. To die with."

Dorothy put her hands on Polvo's chest and pushed him away so she could maintain eye contact.

"Really..?"

"It's always how I've felt. Always. I couldn't imagine myself ever being with anyone different. Not in a million years. If you weren't in my life, I would never want to love again."

"Polvo, why are you saying all this?"

Another moment of silence.

Polvo breathed a shaky sigh as tears welled in his eyes. His lower lip trembled.

"I'm scared, D," he choked out as his tears flushed

down his cheeks. "Gorov's sending us on a mission tomorrow... and I don't know for sure if I'll be making the journey home."

Dorothy brought her hands to her mouth as she gasped. Soon enough, tears of her own formed. "How can you be sure of that?"

Polvo just stared at her for a moment as his tears streamed.

"There was a big fight today... One of ours didn't make it. Gorov didn't even bat an eye at the news."

"That's terrible... I'm so sorry, Polvo," she said, collapsing back into his arms.

"He..." Polvo trembled. "He killed dad..."

Polvo's knees gave out from under him, and the two dropped to the floor. He sat there, sobbing and shaking his head.

"I'm so sorry... I'm so sorry..."

"I thought I hated him all throughout my life. Everything he did wasn't what I wanted. But it was what he thought I needed. And I hated him for it."

Dorothy interrupted the streaks of tears on his cheek with her hand.

"He loved you. He knew you loved him too. And I know you love me, Polvo."

They held each other there for what felt like hours.

As the two slowly died down, and ran out of tears to cry, Dorothy leaned into Polvo's ear.

"I think I'm pregnant, Polvo," she said with her shaky breath.

Polvo's heart seemed to drop into his stomach. He looked up at her and grabbed her shoulders.

"Are you serious, D?"

She nodded.

Polvo's reserve of tears had very suddenly found some spare rations.

A trembling smile broke across Dorothy's face as he let out her breath, her chest still heaving from crying.

Polvo leaned in and kissed her again. As they kissed, they rose back to their feet.

"I promise I'll come back tomorrow. I promise with all my heart I will come back to you."

"I'll remember that," Dorothy smiled brighter.

Despite the exhaustion that riddled his body, Polvo's brain couldn't get a wink of sleep that night.

POLVO WAS THE FIRST at the gate in the morning. Griffin was next, then Piper, then Tony. Despite how little he knew Nori, it still just felt wrong being there without her.

Don Gorov emerged from behind the gate and clapped his huge hands together.

"Big day, big day people. Look alive yeah?" He paused. "Ah… poor choice of words huh?" He chuckled to himself. The Tempest grimaced. "Anyways, get this shit done today, and you'll never need to work a day for me again! Probably. And if you fail, try making like that other one yesterday, and get yourself killed. You won't want to come back with a defeat under your belt anyways."

Polvo watched Griffin ball his fists. It almost felt like Gorov was waiting for something to come. But nothing did.

"Alright. You guys know where the base is, alls you gotta do is storm the place. My extra muscle yesterday took care of a *shit ton* of them, so there shouldn't be an immense amount of them left. We think. So, we still have a little extra *oomph* in there for you guys, if you need it."

Don Gorov gestured up the ramp. "Alright. Off ya go. Make your families proud," he said, suddenly locking eyes with Polvo.

Polvo slowed his walk and let the others walk up a bit more. Turned around to Gorov and stood facing him.

"I'm gonna fucking kill you for what you did."

Don Gorov's eyebrows raised a bit as he cocked his head to the side.

"Quite a mouth," he said as he turned and started to walk away. Polvo gritted his teeth and caught back up with the rest of them.

As they walked up the ramp, they couldn't help but feel miserable. Knowing their boss couldn't care less about one of them dying was admittedly a bit of a let down. They didn't expect much of Don Gorov, but their judgments didn't run *that* low. He was still a human being, after all.

"So, this is probably gonna be it, huh?" Tony broke the Tempest's silence.

"That's what it was sounding like," Polvo said as they

all stared at their feet as they walked. "Because I mean, if we succeed, we just get to live in the Undercity, and if we fail, we'll be dead. Gorov would probably just make another Tempest or something."

"Well, that makes me feel great," Tony tapered off.

As the group reached the door, they did their usual 'coast-is-clear' check, before sealing the door behind them, and starting towards the Sewers base.

Eventually, the group reached the entrance. Everyone looked uncomfortably to Griffin. He looked back at the group behind him. The remainder of the Tempest, accompanied by around 20 armed citizens. He breathed a heavy sigh. Shouldering his metal bat, he began the march into the base.

The setting around them was repulsive, to say the least. Polvo was relieved to be wearing a respirator, because he was certain if he could smell the walls surrounding him, he wouldn't be able to fight, let alone not throw up.

As they all trudged through the increasingly darkened tunnel, Polvo remembered his father's letter. Clutching his coat where the letter sat within the pocket, Polvo closed his eyes. He decided then and there what he wanted to do.

Eventually, the group saw a light at the end of the tunnel. As they approached it, they realized it was a clearing. The center of the Sewer system expanded upwards, in a massive dome that ended with tunnels going deep throughout the underside of the entire city. Candles littered the inside of the base, creating enough light to almost simulate daytime.

"This isn't good," Griffin said uneasily. The Tempest looked at him, confused.

"It's not right," he continued. "We've made it this far without seeing a single other person. They're *letting* us get into the center of their base, so we can't flee as easily."

With Griffin's words, shivered sprinted down the rest of their spines.

And almost directly after he stopped speaking, the group halted at a sound up ahead. Standing tall in the center of the Sewers base, was a crude statue of Filthus, the first Rat King. From behind it, a man walked into view. Polvo recognized the battered crown atop his head.

Nezumi.

"Well, well," he called out, voice echoing through the chambers and tunnels. "It seems we've upset the mighty Tempest with our actions yesterday!" As he exclaimed, chitters and laughs reverberated from all tunnels, causing the Tempest to jump, and stare all around them.

They were surrounded, but they couldn't see anyone yet.

"What concerns me though," Nezumi continued, "is that you have the gall to actually bring your men into our chambers. That's slightly more than slightly frowned upon by us."

"We aren't afraid," Griffin called back. "We've come to finish you off, and we don't intend on leaving without doing so."

"So be it then," Nezumi stopped pacing. Suddenly he raised his arms above his head, and dropped them towards the Tempest.

"Let's get 'em, gentlemen," he said as Rats swarmed the center room.

Polvo already had his sword in hand, but he had the same objective as he did the day before. No blood will be spilled by his hands.

Griffin screamed out a guttural cry as he instantly swung into the closest Rat's stomach. As the man crumpled to the ground, Griffin had already readied another swing, and had taken it.

The rest of the Tempest shrieked as the Sewer flooded with people. Swords clashed against pipes, and the symphony of metal erupted throughout the subterranean lair.

Polvo fought a few Rats back with the butte of his sword, but as soon as a clearing was made, he sprinted in the direction of Nezumi. Jumping onto the pedestal that he was standing atop before, Polvo strained his eyes, searching for the Rat King. His eyes caught on the crown as he watched the King triumphantly marching down one of the tunnel paths.

Jumping from the statue's base, Polvo ducked a few attacks, and pushed his way through the surging crowd. Ducking a few attacks, and shoving bodies into one another, he eventually forced his way out, and bolted down the tunnel Nezumi had previously walked.

As he ran, Polvo followed the trail of pocket change, when he eventually reached a door.

In a sewer system full of the same iron grid door, the ornately carved wooden door caught him off guard. It wasn't fully closed, and he could see the bright firelight shining through the crack. Taking a deep breath, Polvo pushed the door open and walked in.

"Close the door behind you, please," Nezumi said from under his desk. Polvo could hear him rifling through the drawers.

Confused, Polvo closed the door behind him.

"Thanks, man. Got a massive headache from all that noise. Had to keep up the character though, huh?"

Polvo sheathed his sword as he walked further into the room.

"You know I was coming in here with the impression and intention of killing you?"

"Yeah. Hope you don't still do that though," Nezumi said as he continued under his desk. "Listen, Polvo, I don't have anything in here for you to fight. To be honest, I don't think you want to fight either, considering how fast you sheathed your weapon."

"Good assumption," Polvo said as he relaxed.

"Take a seat, I'll be up in a second," Nezumi said, before making a distinct '*aha!*' sound, and popping his head up from the desk.

Polvo sat down in one of the dilapidated chairs in front of the desk, and Nezumi jumped up onto the throne, with a piece of paper in hand.

"What's this all about Nezumi? How did you know my name?"

"I know a lot about you, Polvo. Actually, we're closer than you think," he said as he unfolded the paper. He tossed it onto the desk, and Polvo hesitantly grabbed onto it. He gasped at the handwriting.

"Your father Travis," Nezumi started while Polvo frantically read the letter. "Was a dear friend of mine in my youth. He actually saved my life, believe it or not. He disappeared one day with the Undercity project underway. This was what he left me."

⟫◆⟪

Piper ducked just in time, as the metal pipe flew over her head, and eventually collided with another Sewers member. She barely had time to suck in breath before having to roll out of the way of another strike. She slashed out with a dagger, letting loose the crimson ribbons from a Rat's leg. He wailed as he hit the ground, and Piper darted through the crowd.

Griffin screamed as his muscles strained under the force of him swinging. Cleaving through multiple Rats with one swing of his bat, he couldn't feel the tears streaming down his face.

Tony was face down towards the back of the battle, trying desperately not to be caught playing dead.

As the clash of metal and skin continued, Piper looked around for Polvo. Nowhere to be seen, she continued darting around the battlefield. As the war continued, the sound of bodies hitting the floor rattled throughout the sewer system. Piper cried as she ducked more attacks, one eventually clipping her arm. She cried out as the pipe smashed into her bicep as hard as the Rat could swing it. Piper collapsed to the ground, and looked up at the Rats surrounding her.

Griffin saw the pileup and sprinted. Shoulder first, he slammed into a Rat, sending him flying across the room. He planted his front foot and swung through the crowd. Cleaving one Rat's head, Griffin watched the body crumple to the ground beneath the rest of the Sewers members.

⋘◆⋙

"Listen, Polvo," Nezumi said as he stood and started pacing around the room. "This fight isn't ending anywhere near well for your side. The Rats I have out there aren't even half of the entire gang. We have reserves all throughout the tunnels down here. They're just waiting for the King's command, and they'll swarm. I'm telling you, there's only one way this ends. I'm sorry."

"Why..." Polvo started. "Why do you want to do this?"

"I'm tired man," he breathed as he stopped pacing. "I've been King for what... ten years now? Look, I know Filthus died in this position, but that's really just not something I'm willing to do. I want to settle down in the Calm Waters. Maybe buy a house, I don't know."

"You're actually serious…" Polvo said, staring down at his lap.

"Yeah, kid. I am."

"But that would mean I couldn't…"

"Yup. Can't go home. Can't really do anything. That's kinda the gig."

"What about someone on the Surface?"

"Risky. I wouldn't want to be showing your face much. If Gorov keeps his word, there'll be another Tempest after yours. Anyone sees that mug, you and anyone you associate with will be dead."

"Wait, then how would I be..?"

"Thought of that, actually. I made this," Nezumi said as he grabbed something from his desk drawer. Holding it up, it was a respirator. Similar to the model Polvo had, it covered his entire head, and the front was modified to look like the head of a rat.

Polvo reached out and took the mask. "You're really serious."

"As the plague," Nezumi said. "What do you say?"

Polvo stared down at the respirator in front of him. Nezumi reached up and took the golden crown from his head, and placed it on the table.

⋘◆⋙

Griffin's muscles screamed as he blasted his bat through another member of the Sewers. Piper hadn't gotten up yet. As Griffin cleared through the Rats that still surrounded her, he belted out a deafening scream as he pushed his muscles past their limits. It had to end there. He had to end it there.

And with that thought fresh in his mind, the back of his skull was caved in.

The Rat behind him held the newly bloodied pipe, and watched Griffin fall limply to the ground. The battlefield seemed to quiet as he fell. Heads turned, and clashes ceased. Some of Gorov's paid civilians bolted through the tunnel they had initially walked through.

And with that, it had seemed the Tempest was dead.

POLVO STOOD ABOVE PIPER. The breath that rocked her body up and down was weak and slow. Kneeling down, Polvo turned her so she could see him. Her eyes didn't widen until he took off his new respirator.

"P-Polvo…" She managed to choke out. Polvo shook his head and tapped his index finger over his lips. She grew silent again.

"What was her name?" Polvo said, tears welling in his eyes. "The girl you dug that tunnel to see."

Piper smiled weakly at the thought of her.

"M-Moros…" she choked out. "S-She's… my niece…"

Polvo remembered the name and nodded to her. He held her there as the light left her eyes, and the soul left the body.

Laying the body down again, Polvo secured his mask, and marched to the statue of Filthus in the center of the room. The members of the Sewers were silent.

"Nezumi is gone," he bellowed into the crowd. "And in his wake, he left me. The reign of the Masked Rat King begins *NOW*."

The crowd suddenly broke into applause. Polvo raised his arms above his head and breathed in the electricity in the air. As the applause slowly died down, Polvo dropped his arms to his sides.

"Today, we mourn the losses of this battle, and we cleanse our home of their bodies they've left behind. But tomorrow," he said, grinning ear to ear under his mask. "Tomorrow, we start planning a factory takedown."

Applause once more, this time significantly more deafening than the last.

As Polvo and the other members of the Sewers began cleaning and removing the bodies, he came across Tony. Like he felt when he saw Griffin, Polvo felt regret that he couldn't be there to see it happen. To hear a final goodbye. And as Polvo started this sad train of thought, Tony rolled over, with his gauntlets up.

"Okay, sir, I'm so sorry, but I'm not dead. Please don't change that, I promise to leave and never bother you again, pinky swear."

Polvo stared at him long and hard, before eventually breaking out into laughter. Standing up, he held a hand out, and helped the remaining Tempest member to his feet once more.

"Gorov's not gonna let you go back, y'know," Polvo said as he watched Tony jerk his head towards him.

"How do you know about him?!"

Polvo lifted up his mask.

"*POLVO?*" Tony exclaimed, before quickly covering his own mouth. "Sorry..."

"It's fine," Polvo chuckled as he dusted off Tony's coat. "Listen though, man, Gorov's gonna have another gang up here within the next couple weeks, no doubt. You can't go back to the Undercity, and you can't stay up here. I think..."

"I gotta leave Arkoma, huh?" Tony stared down at his shoes. "Shit, man..."

"I'll prepare food rations and give you plenty of supplies," Polvo said as he pulled the mask down once more. "But that's it man. I hope you find something out there."

"Thanks," Tony spoke absentmindedly as he thought about what lied outside the borders of Arkoma. "It's been real, Polvo."

"For me, I think it just now got that way," Polvo replied as he pat Tony on the back. "C'mon. Let's get you packing," he said as he led Tony to his new Royal chambers.

EPILOGUE

Dorothy Vorgund sat behind the counter of her shop. It had been another hard day for her, but as she heard someone walk into the shop, she did her best to rub the dried tears from her cheeks.

It had been four years since she heard from Polvo.

She looked through the stands of the shop and saw the silhouette slowly walking through, browsing the inventory.

"If you have any questions, I'm up here," she called out, and looked down at the counter in front of her.

Suddenly, there was a tug at her pant leg. Looking down, she saw her daughter, Shora, smiling up at her.

"Aw, come here," she said under her breath as she picked her daughter up. She stood there for a moment, cradling Shora and smiling, when the customer came to the front of the store.

Looking up, Dorothy gasped lightly, and put Shora down.

"How may I help you, sir?" She said hesitantly as she stared at the Masked Rat King.

He froze for a second, before breathing out, and speaking with a shaky voice.

"Your daughter is beautiful..." he said, trying his best to keep his composure.

Dorothy chuckled and looked down at Shora. "Yes, thank you... She looks just like her father," she said, choking back tears.

The Masked Rat King reached into his trench coat, and pulled two things from his pockets. An adult respirator, and one small enough to fit a child.

Dorothy gasped and covered her mouth with her hands.

"I can't accept these, sir, I don't have anything to pay..."

The Rat King pushed the masks onto the counter towards Dorothy. As he did, he reached up and grabbed his own mask. As he pulled it up and over his face, he spoke.

"Her father would want you two to have them."

ABOUT THE AUTHOR

Photo Credit: Justin DeFreitas

Alex Leverette is a writer. He hopes.

Hailing from Southern California, Alex currently resides in Oregon, where he writes at local coffee shops everyday, and dreams of owning a 1983 DeLorean DMC-12. This story is a spin-off from Industory Studios' audio drama podcast, *The Arkoma Chapters*. Leverette is the lead writer on the project, and even provides voice talents for the main character, Ron Barton.

Alex Leverette is stoked that you read his first book.

"There's more where this came from guys. Just you wait."